FACTIVITY

AMAZING
BODY
Sticker Activity

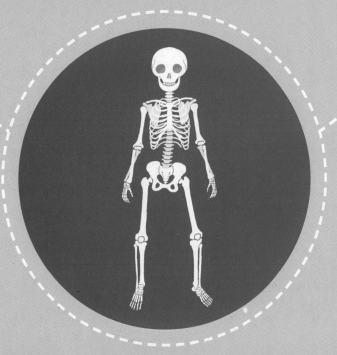

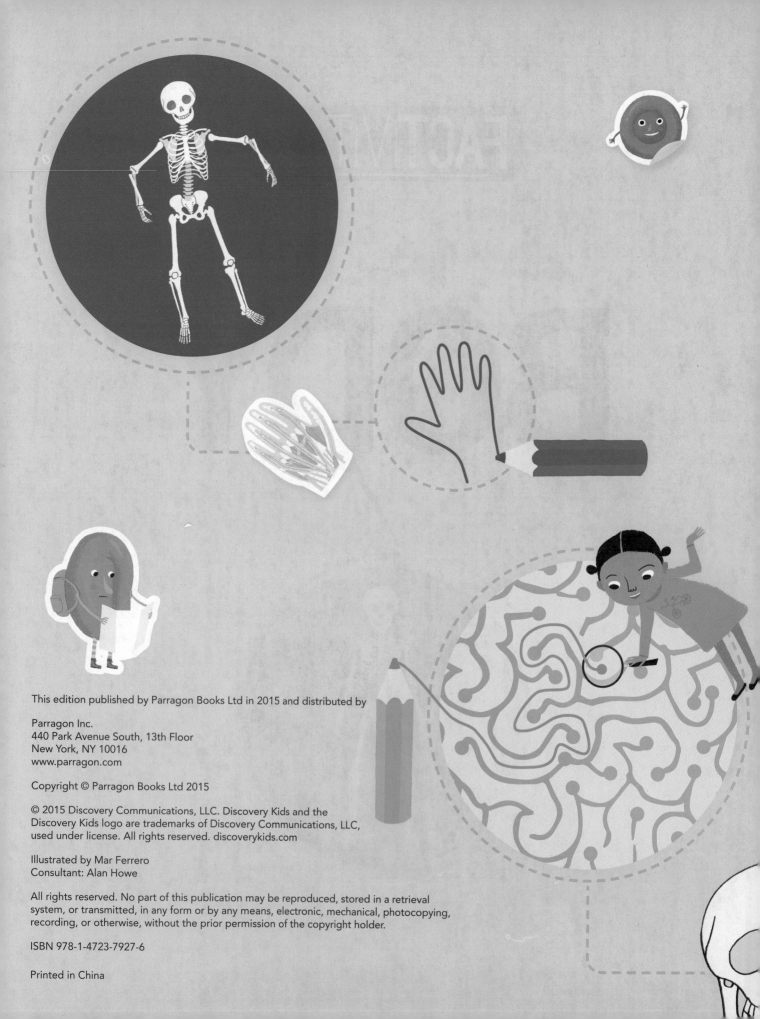

This edition published by Parragon Books Ltd in 2015 and distributed by

Parragon Inc.
440 Park Avenue South, 13th Floor
New York, NY 10016
www.parragon.com

Illustrated by Mar Ferrero
Consultant: Alan Howe

ISBN 978-1-4723-7927-6

Printed in China

FACTIVITY

AMAZING
BODY
Sticker Activity

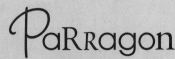

Parragon

Bath · New York · Cologne · Melbourne · Delhi
Hong Kong · Shenzhen · Singapore · Amsterdam

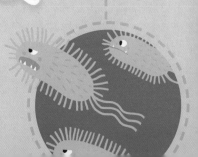

Meet your body

Your body is full of cool stuff, from strong bones to tiny blood cells. Some body parts have special jobs and are called organs.
Add stickers to the organ shapes.

Your **small intestine** takes the goodness from your food.

Your **kidneys** turn waste water into pee.

Your **stomach** turns the food you eat into glop.

Your **heart** pumps blood around your body.

Your **bladder** stores pee.

Your **brain** sends out signals to make your body move, walk, or talk.

Your **lungs** take oxygen from the air you breathe.

Your large intestine collects the waste from your food.

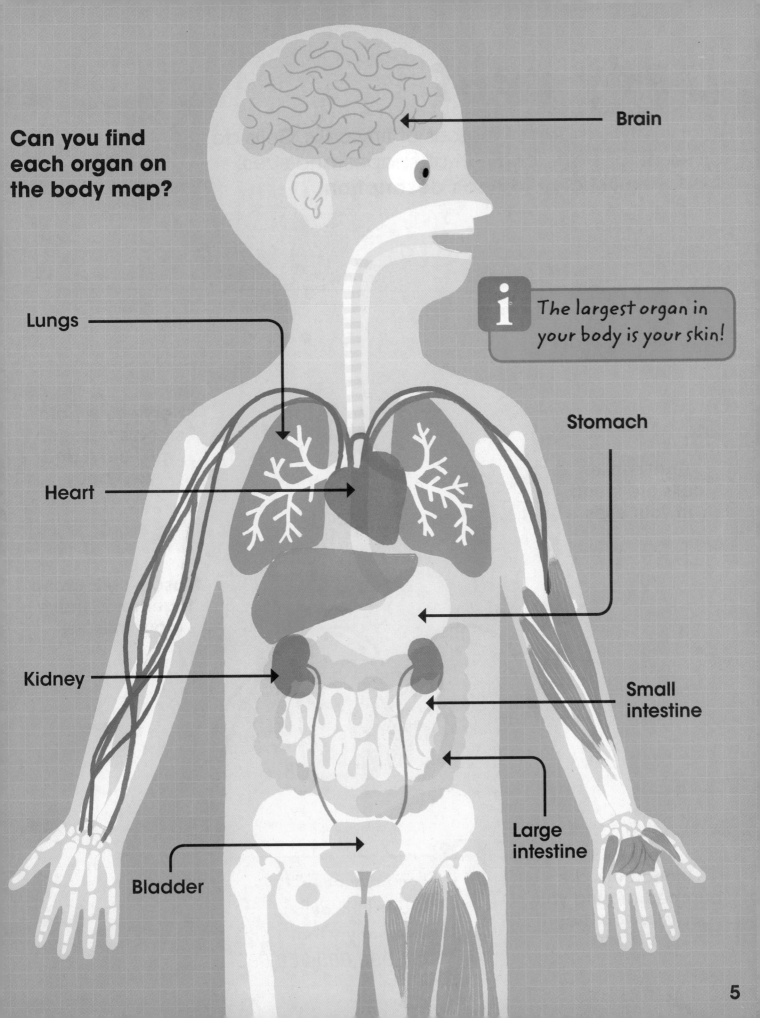

Can you find each organ on the body map?

Brain

Lungs

The largest organ in your body is your skin!

Heart

Stomach

Kidney

Small intestine

Large intestine

Bladder

Body cells

Your body is made of masses of tiny cells. Cells do different jobs and come in all shapes and sizes.
Add a cell sticker to each description.

Light sensor cells are found in your eyes.

Nerve cells carry signals between your brain and your body.

Muscle cells group together to make your muscles.

Blood cells are pumped around your body by your heart.

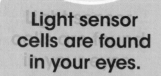
You have about 100 trillion cells in your body—that's 100,000,000,000,000!

Play three in a row with red and white blood cells.

Pick your color, then take turns to add blood cell stickers—the first player to get three in a row wins!

 Red blood cell

 White blood cell

Game 1

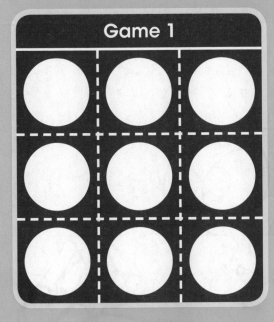

Game 2

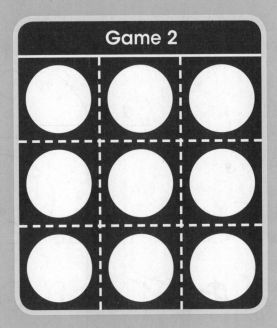

Game 3

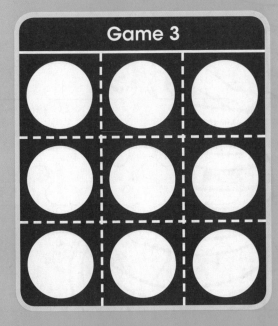

Write the winner of each game here. Add a trophy sticker when you've played all three!

1. ....

2. ....

3. ....

Strong skeleton

Your skeleton is made up of strong bones, which give your body its shape and allow you to move. **Add a skeleton sticker and complete the puzzle with your stickers.**

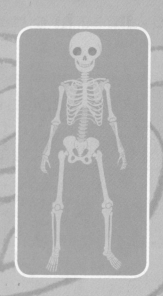

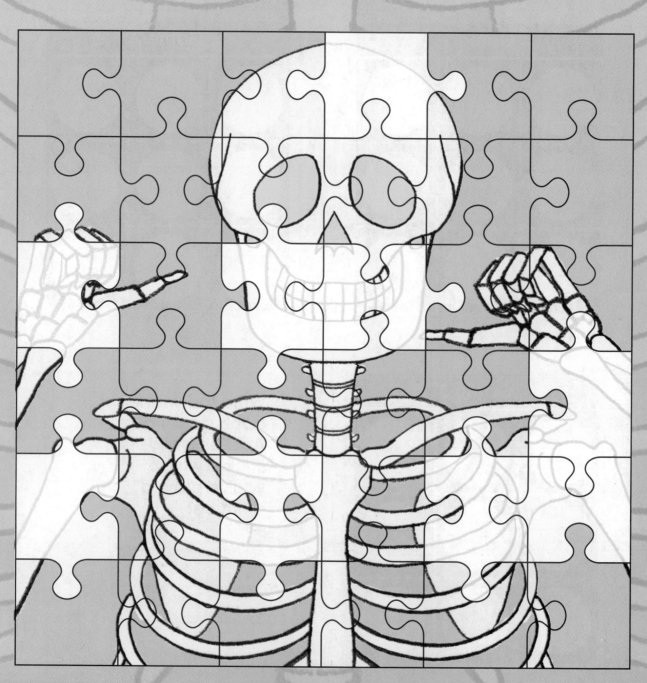

Bony parts

Doctors use X-rays to take pictures of your bones!
Add stickers to these X-ray pictures.

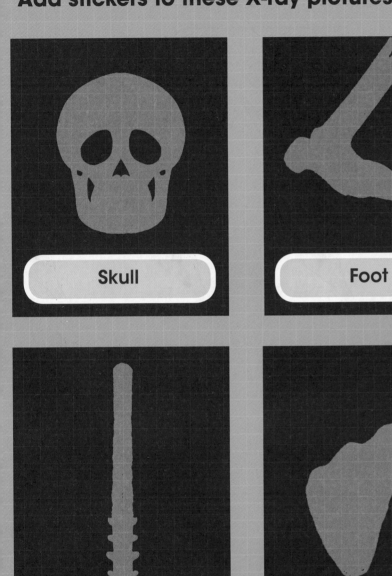

Skull

Foot

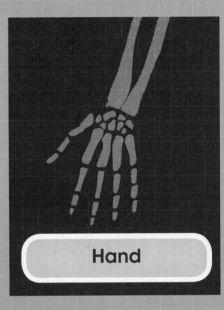

Hand

Backbone

Shoulder

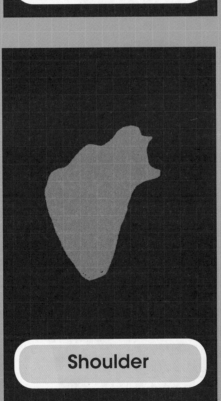

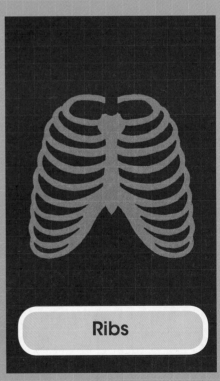

Ribs

i There are more than 200 bones in your body!

Mighty muscles

Muscles provide the power for everything from moving to blinking! They are made up of lots of tiny muscle cells. **Doodle and color lots more here.**

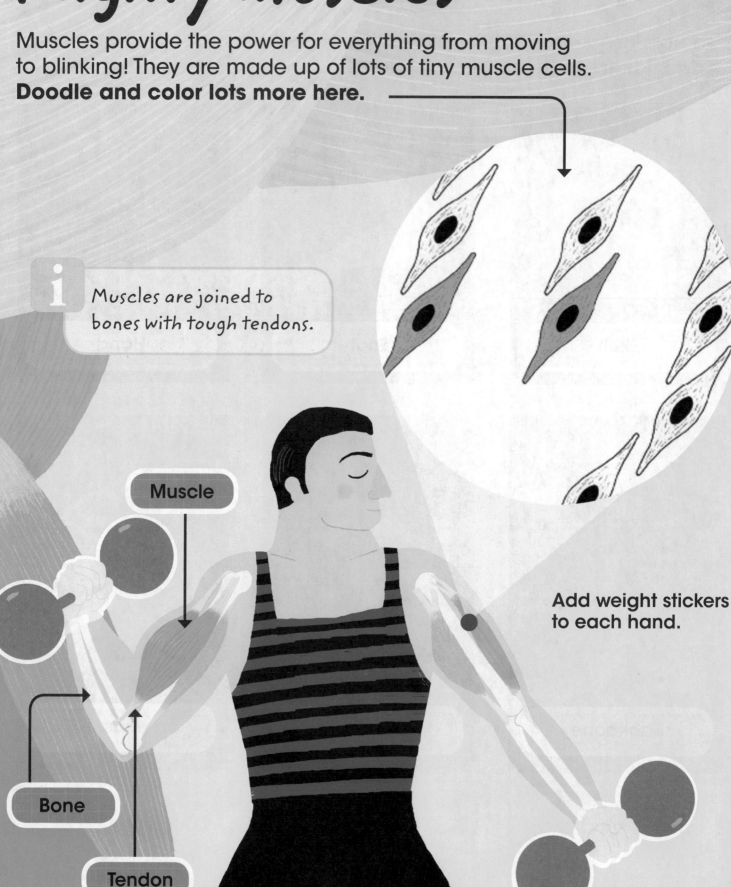

i Muscles are joined to bones with tough tendons.

Muscle

Add weight stickers to each hand.

Bone

Tendon

Muscles don't just help you move around. **Find a sticker for each of these muscles that do special jobs.**

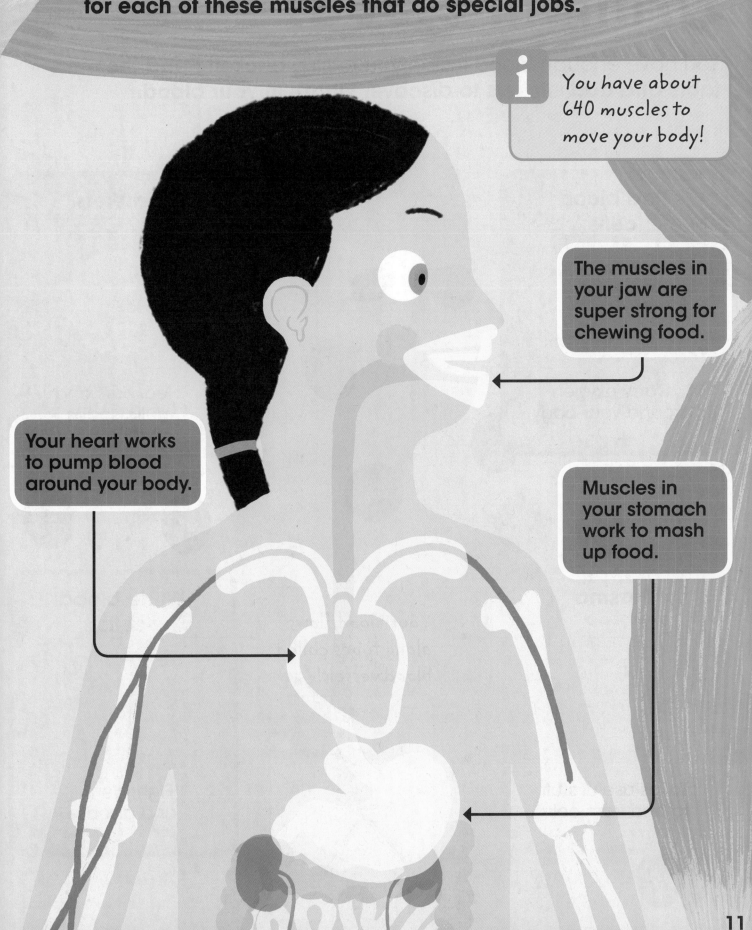

i You have about 640 muscles to move your body!

The muscles in your jaw are super strong for chewing food.

Your heart works to pump blood around your body.

Muscles in your stomach work to mash up food.

Brilliant blood

You have enough blood inside you to fill a bucket! **Read the facts and add stickers to discover what's in your blood.**

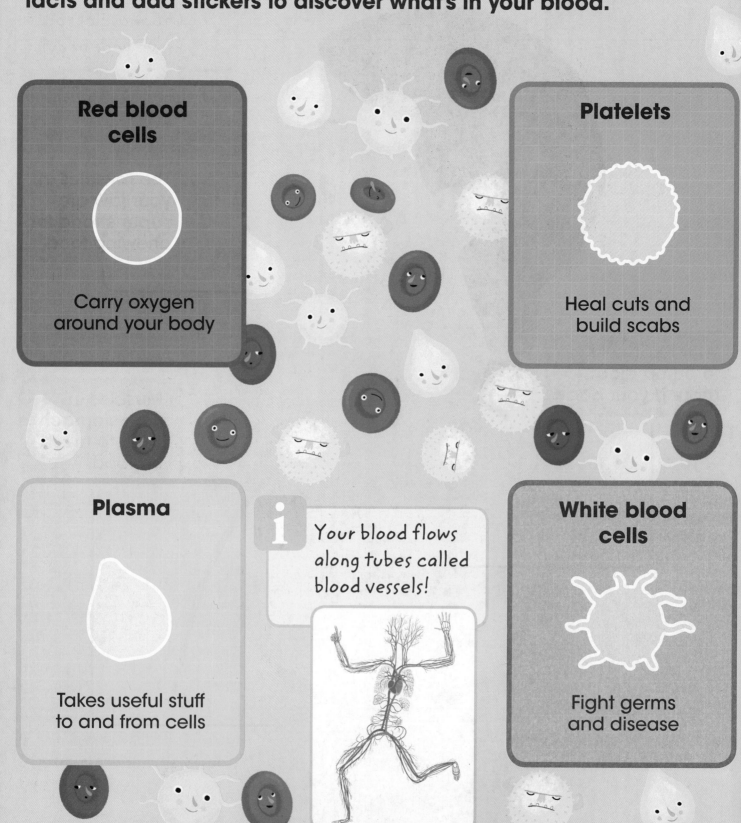

Red blood cells

Carry oxygen around your body

Platelets

Heal cuts and build scabs

Plasma

Takes useful stuff to and from cells

Your blood flows along tubes called blood vessels!

White blood cells

Fight germs and disease

Your blood carries everything you need around your body.
Follow the tubes to discover what blood delivers and collects.

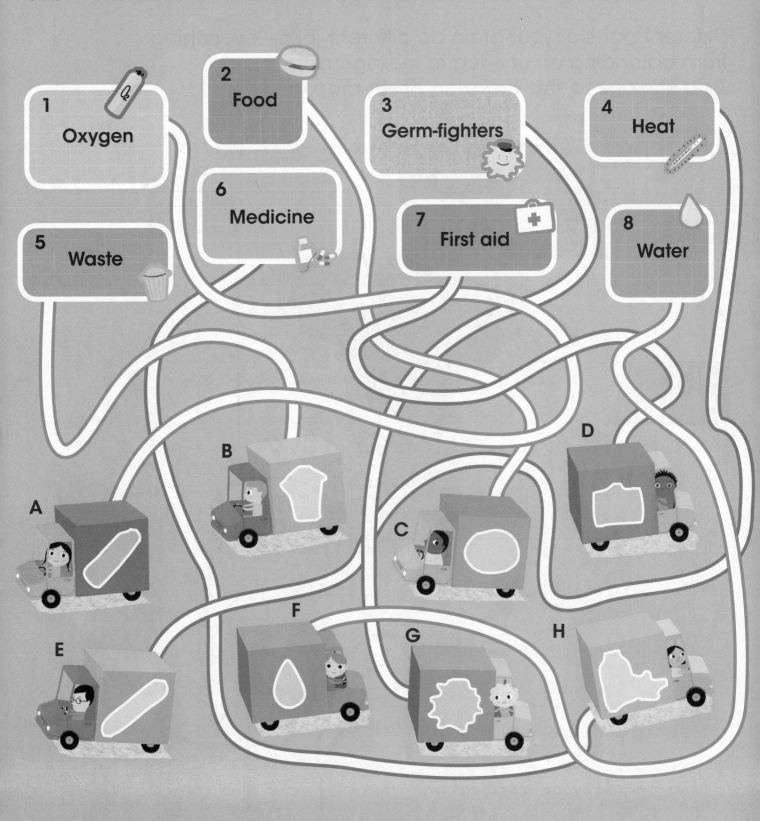

1 Oxygen

2 Food

3 Germ-fighters

4 Heat

6 Medicine

5 Waste

7 First aid

8 Water

A

B

C

D

E

F

G

H

Add a sticker on each van to show what blood carries.

Your brain

Different parts of your brain do different jobs—everything from balancing on one leg to feeling happy or sad!
Add stickers to this amazing brain map.

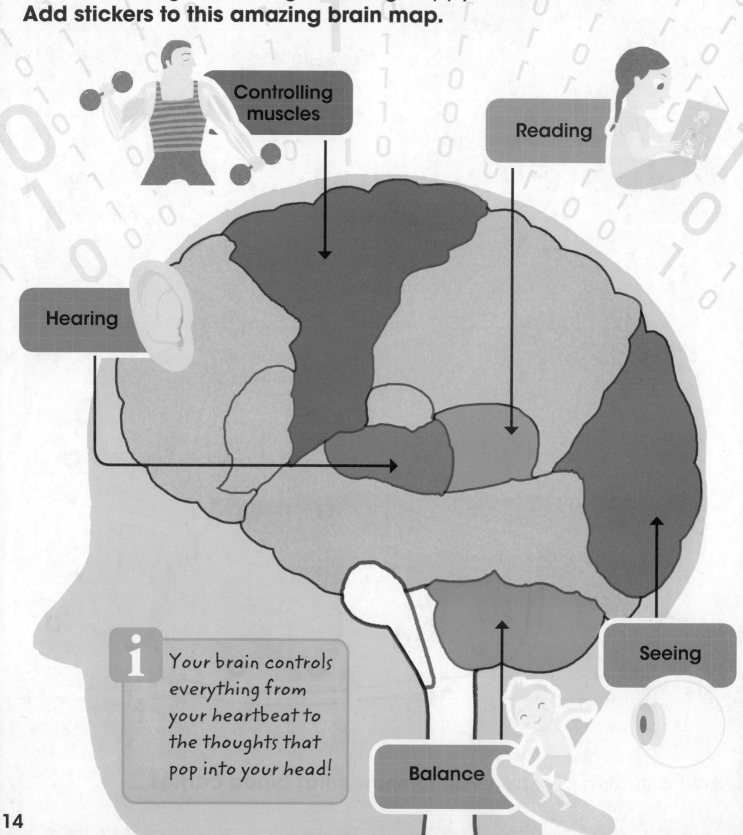

Controlling muscles

Reading

Hearing

Seeing

i Your brain controls everything from your heartbeat to the thoughts that pop into your head!

Balance

Brain power

Your brain can handle thousands of pieces of information every second. **Put your brain through its paces and complete these puzzles as quickly as you can!**

1. Write how many rabbits you can count.

2. Circle the odd one out.

3. Draw the next shape to complete the pattern.

4. Draw lines to match up the colors.

5. Connect the dots to complete the picture.

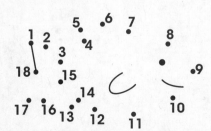

Fantastic food

Food is the body's fuel. Different foods contain different things—your body needs all of them to stay healthy.
Add food stickers to the plate.

Water keeps your cells and blood healthy.

Proteins help your body grow and repair itself.

Carbohydrates provide you with energy.

Vitamins and minerals keep your bones and blood cells strong.

Fats help you store energy and keep warm.

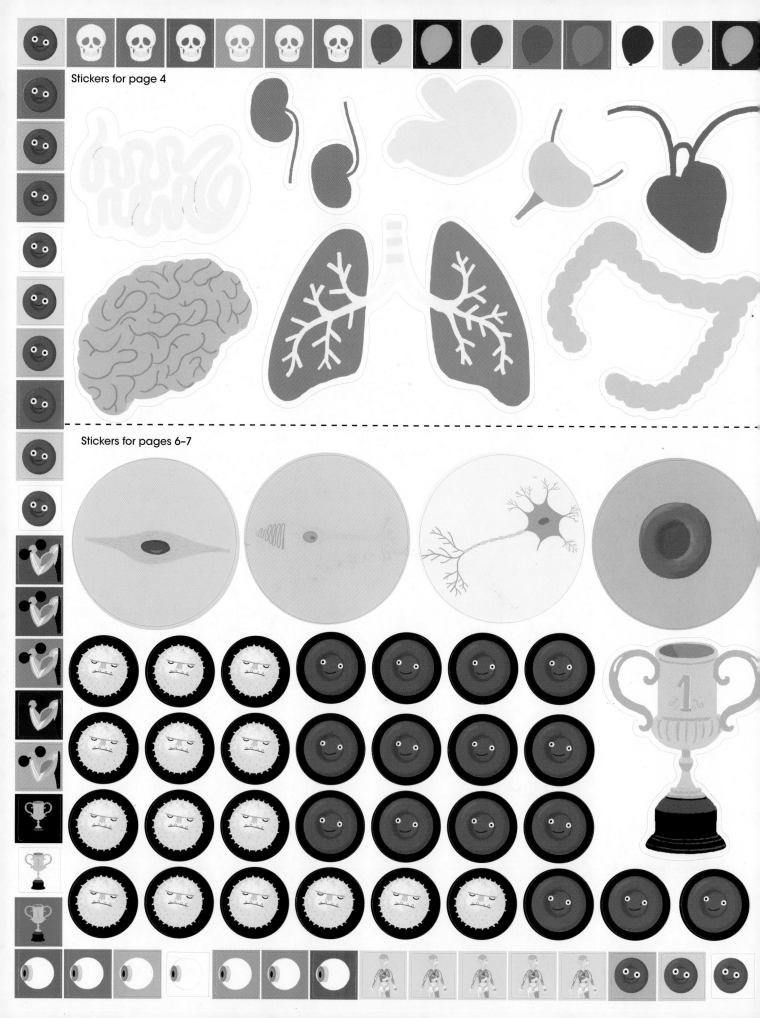

Stickers for page 4

Stickers for pages 6–7

Stickers for pages 8–9

Stickers for pages 10–11

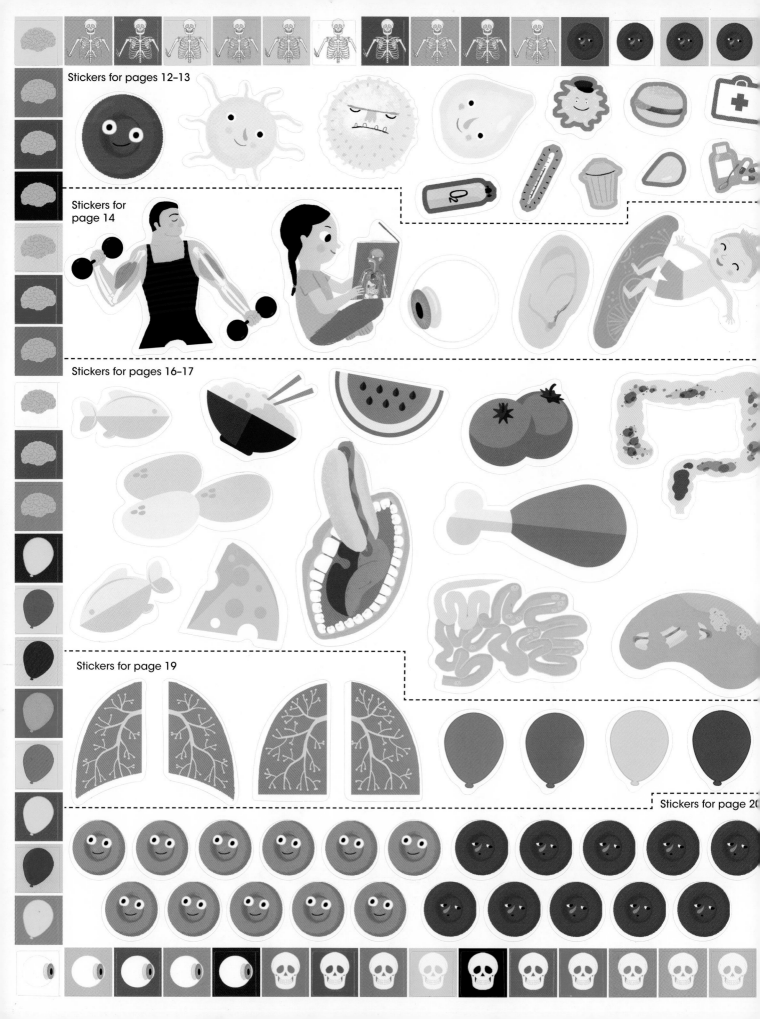

Stickers for pages 12–13

Stickers for page 14

Stickers for pages 16–17

Stickers for page 19

Stickers for page 20

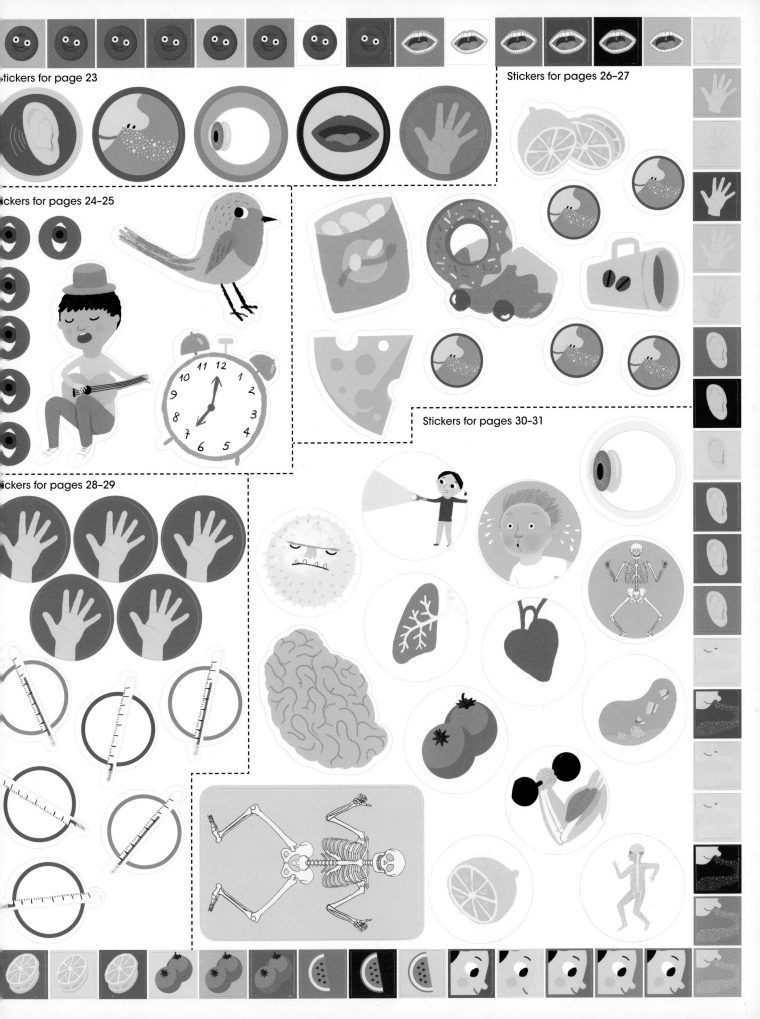

stickers for page 23

Stickers for pages 26–27

Stickers for pages 24–25

Stickers for pages 30–31

Stickers for pages 28–29

The food journey

Before you can use the food you eat, it has to be broken down in your digestive system. **Add stickers to discover each stage of the food journey.**

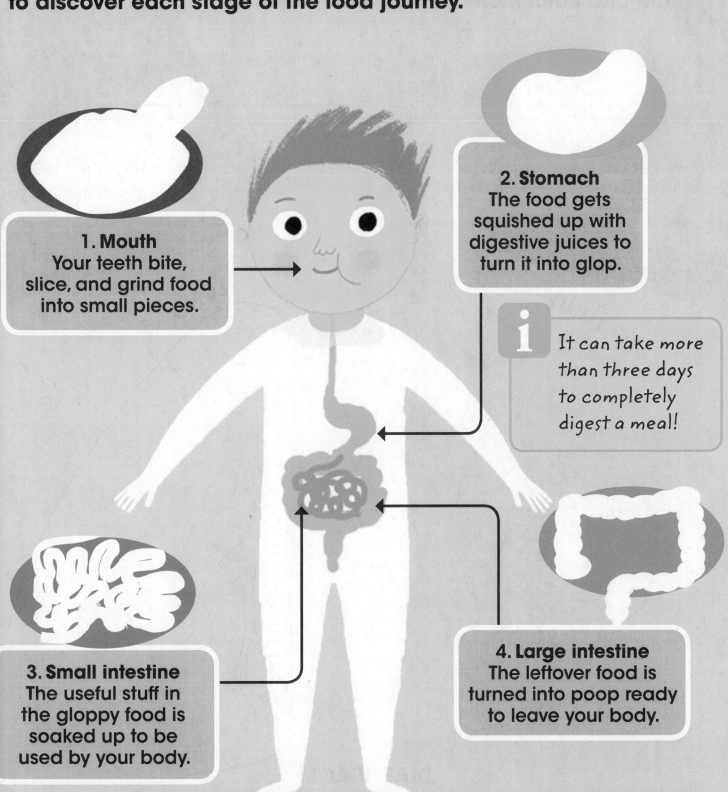

1. Mouth
Your teeth bite, slice, and grind food into small pieces.

2. Stomach
The food gets squished up with digestive juices to turn it into glop.

i It can take more than three days to completely digest a meal!

3. Small intestine
The useful stuff in the gloppy food is soaked up to be used by your body.

4. Large intestine
The leftover food is turned into poop ready to leave your body.

Breathtaking!

Your body needs a gas called oxygen. Oxygen passes into your blood from your lungs whenever you breathe in. **Doodle and color more tubes to complete the lung.**

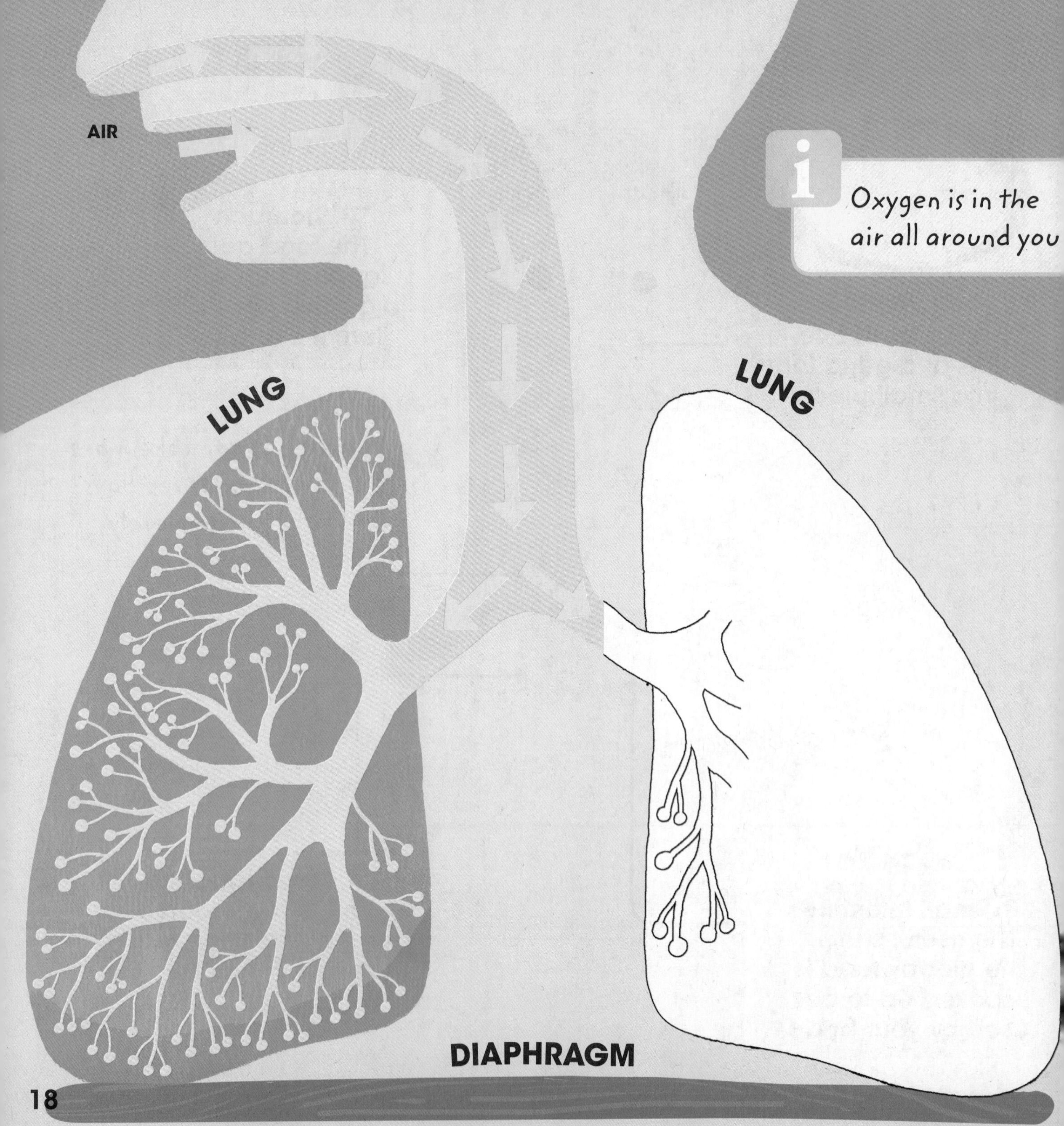

AIR

i

Oxygen is in the air all around you

LUNG

LUNG

DIAPHRAGM

Your diaphragm is a strong muscle that helps you breathe.
Add the lung stickers to each picture.

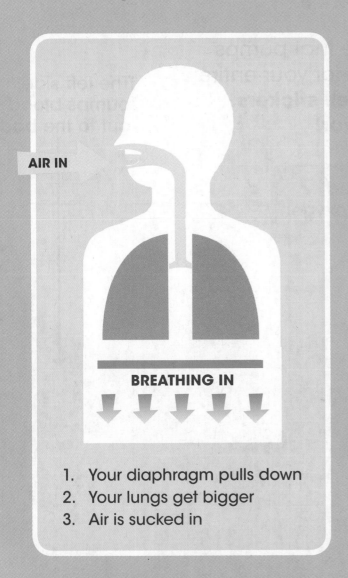

AIR IN

BREATHING IN

1. Your diaphragm pulls down
2. Your lungs get bigger
3. Air is sucked in

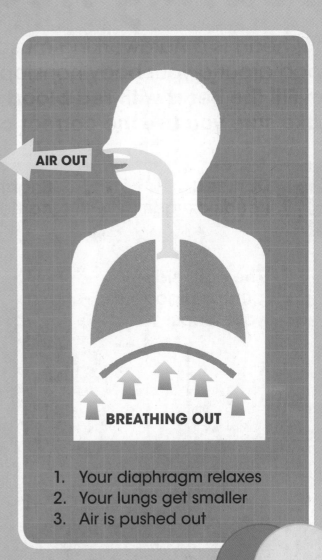

AIR OUT

BREATHING OUT

1. Your diaphragm relaxes
2. Your lungs get smaller
3. Air is pushed out

Add a different color balloon to each fact!

Some people can hold their breath for over ten minutes!

Hairs inside your nose keep dust and dirt from getting into your lungs.

You breathe out a gas called carbon dioxide.

You breathe through your nose as well as your mouth!

Beating heart

Your heart is a hardworking muscle that pumps blood around your body nonstop—for your entire life! **Fill the heart with red blood cell stickers. Make sure you use the correct color!**

Dark red needs oxygen

Bright red carries oxygen

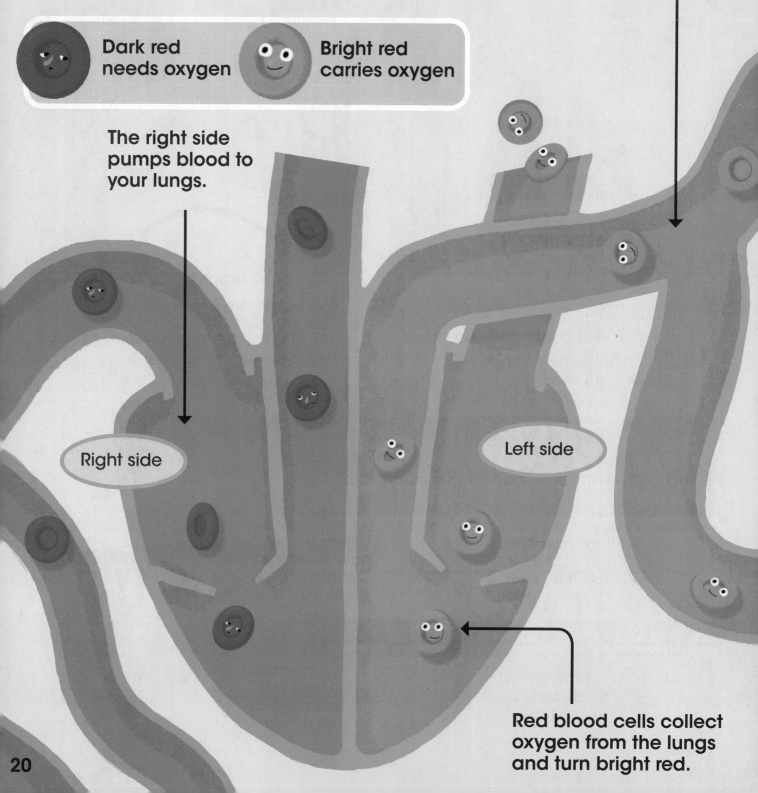

The left side pumps blood out to the body.

The right side pumps blood to your lungs.

Right side

Left side

Red blood cells collect oxygen from the lungs and turn bright red.

Exercise time!

When you exercise, your heart pumps faster to get blood to your cells more quickly. **Draw yourself doing some exercise that makes your heart race.**

football   skipping   walking dog   running   swimming

Sending messages

Your nervous system carries messages between your brain and body. **Follow the nerve path to find out where this brain is sending a message!**

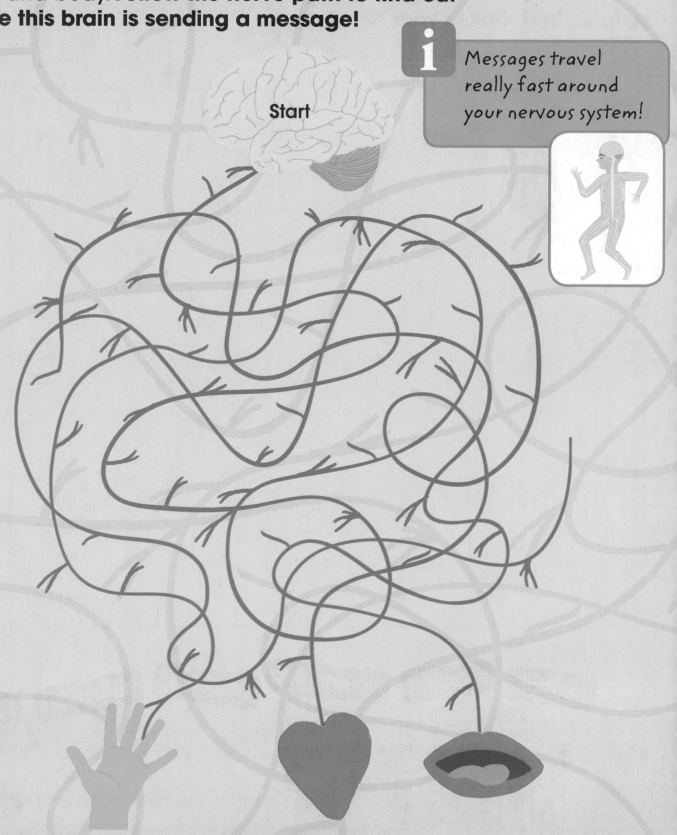

Start

i Messages travel really fast around your nervous system!

Super senses

Your senses tell your brain all about the world so it can decide what to do. **Add the correct sense sticker to each picture!**

Your senses

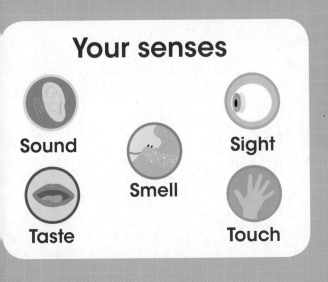

- **Sound**
- **Smell**
- **Sight**
- **Taste**
- **Touch**

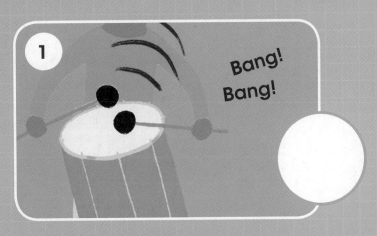

1 Bang! Bang!

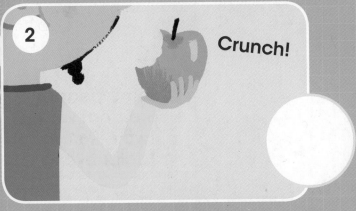

2 Crunch!

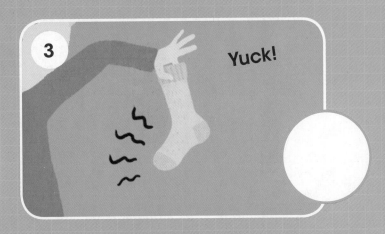

3 Yuck!

4 Hmm!

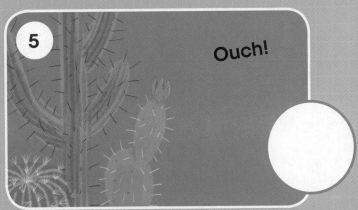

5 Ouch!

Eyes and ears

Your eyes take millions of pictures and send them to your brain.
Add an eye sticker to each fact and the things this eye can see!

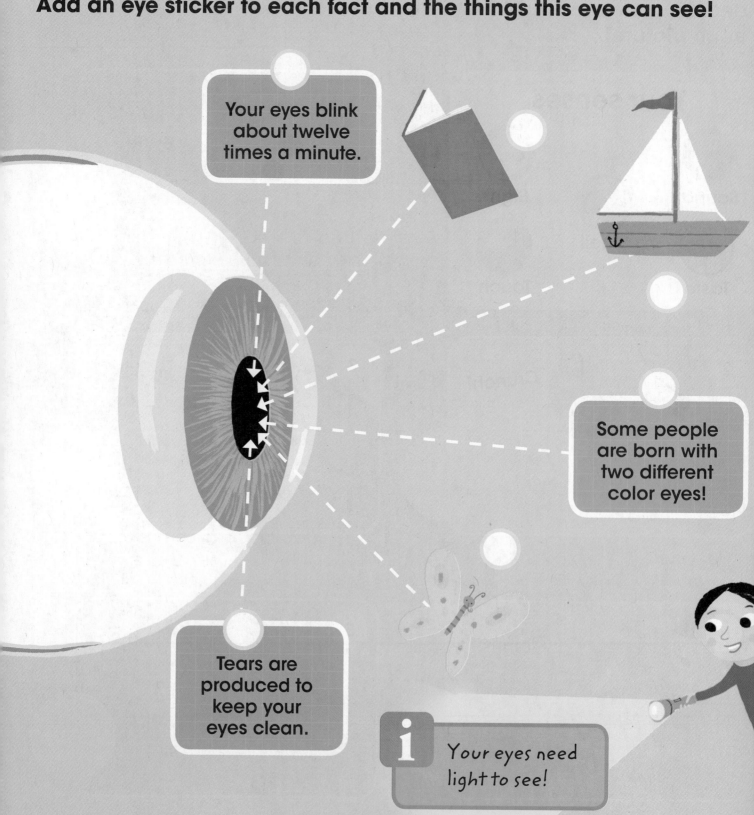

Your eyes blink about twelve times a minute.

Some people are born with two different color eyes!

Tears are produced to keep your eyes clean.

i Your eyes need light to see!

Sounds travel through the air to your ears, which turn them into signals that your brain can understand. **Use the sound clues to add noisy stickers below!**

Tweet tweet!

Ring ring!

Twang twang!

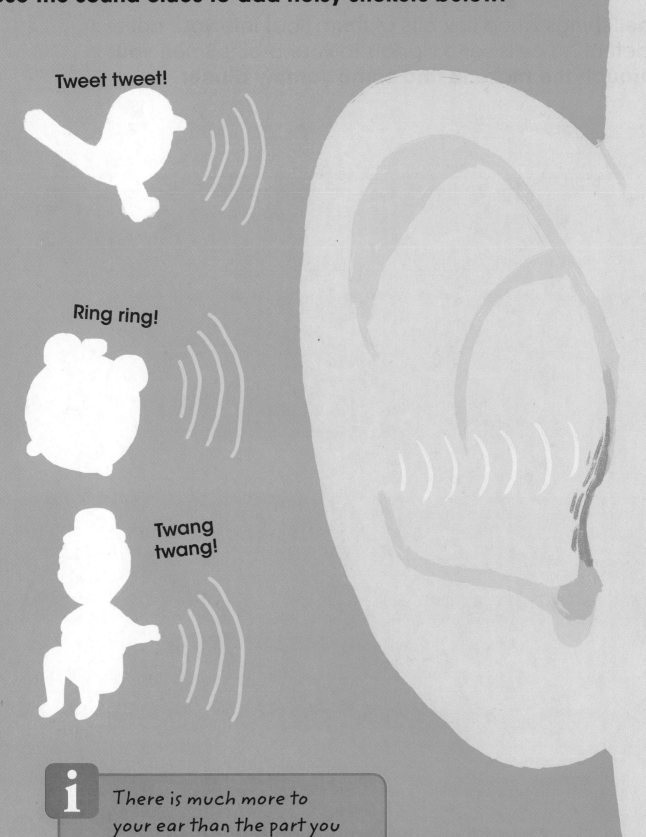

i There is much more to your ear than the part you see outside your head!

Follow your nose!

You smell things when tiny bits of them float into your nose. Smell detecting cells send signals to your brain! **Smell your way through the maze to find some yummy dinner.**

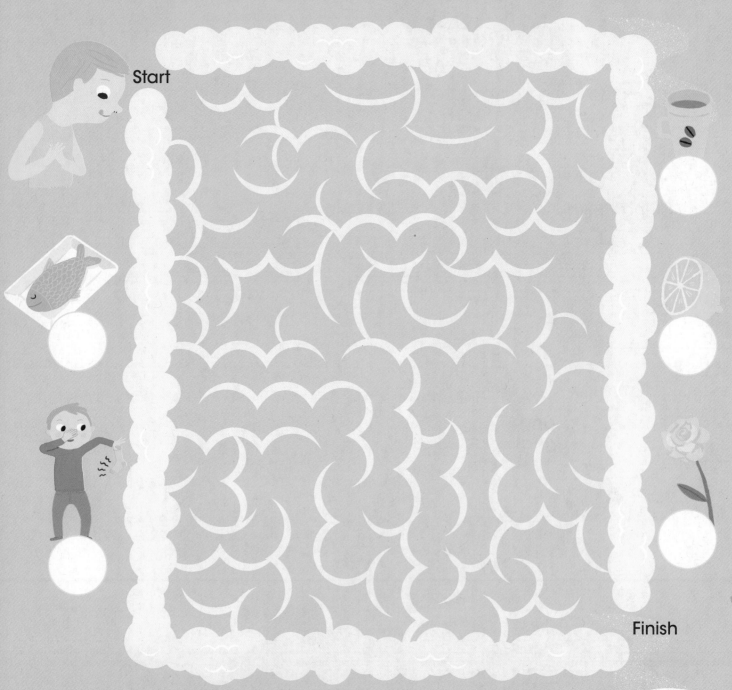

Start

Finish

Count five other smells on this page. Add a nose sticker next to each one!

Tasty treats

Your tongue tastes everything you eat or drink! There are five main tastes it can sense. **Complete this picture by adding the correct food sticker to each plate.**

Potato chips are salty

Cake is sweet

Lemons are sour

Cheese is umami

Coffee is bitter

ℹ Your tongue has about 10,000 taste buds!

Touch and feel

Touch sensors in your skin tell you whether things are soft, hard, rough, or smooth. **Color the picture and add a hand sticker to each person touching something!**

Hot and cold

Your body can sense whether things are hot or cold, too.
**Add a blue thermometer sticker to things that feel cold
and a red one to things that feel hot.**

i You sweat to cool down when you're hot
and shiver to warm up when you're cold!

Amazing body sticker quiz

Now that you know all about your amazing body, try this sticker quiz!
Check the answer, then find a matching sticker.

You can find all the answers in this book!

3. Your brain remembers all these facts! Stick a picture here.

1. Where would you find a light sensor cell?

A) Brain ☐
B) Eyes ☐
C) Hair ☐

4. What is your heart made of?

A) Bone ☐
B) Fat ☐
C) Muscle ☐

2. How many bones are joined together to make your skeleton?

A) Over 20 ☐
B) Over 200 ☐
C) Over 2000 ☐

5. Which food group gives you strong bones and blood cells?

A) Proteins ☐
B) Vitamins and minerals ☐
C) Water ☐

6. Where is food mixed with digestive juices and turned into glop?

A) Stomach ☐
B) Kidney ☐
C) Large intestine ☐

7. What does your body need to do when it's too hot?

A) Sweat ☐
B) Shiver ☐
C) Sleep ☐

8. Which cells in your blood fight germs and disease?

A) Red blood cells ☐
B) Blue blood cells ☐
C) White blood cells ☐

9. Find a skeleton sticker to put here.

10. How many muscles do you have to move your body?

A) 6 ☐
B) 64 ☐
C) 640 ☐

11. Which organ fills with air when you breathe in?

A) Lung ☐
B) Bladder ☐
C) Heart ☐

12. What system carries messages around your body?

A) Digestive system ☐
B) Nervous system ☐
C) Worried system ☐

13. What do your eyes need to be able to see?

A) Light ☐
B) Air ☐
C) Sound waves ☐

14. Which of these foods tastes sour?

A) Chocolate ☐
B) Banana ☐
C) Lemon ☐

31

Answers

Page 8

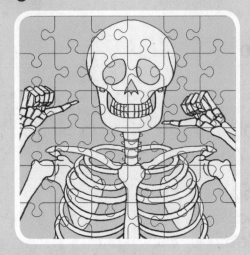

Page 13
A–1, B–5, C–2, D–7,
E–4, F–8, G–3, H–6

Page 15
1. Seven

2.

3.

Page 22
The brain is sending a
message to the hand.

Page 23

Page 26

Page 29

Pages 30–31

1. B
2. B
3.

4. C
5. B
6. A
7. A
8. C

9.
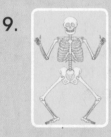

10. C
11. A
12. B
13. A
14. C